Susan Thompson

THE TWO-WHEELED DETECTIVE

Susan Thompson spent twenty years in the adult literacy field as a teacher, program director, curriculum developer, trainer, and mentor to adult literacy professionals. Susan is a graduate of Hollins University, the New School Certificate Program in adult literacy, and a recipient of the 2011 Literacy Recognition Award from the New York City Literacy Assistance Center. She lives in Brooklyn, New York.

Susan is a lifelong reader of mystery stories and is delighted to introduce you to Tami Tripper.

First published by Gemma in 2023.

www.gemmamedia.org

©2023 by Susan Thompson

All rights reserved. No part of this publication may be reproduced in any manner whatsoever without written permission from the publisher, except in the case of brief quotations embodied in critical articles or reviews.

Printed in the United States of America

978-1-956476-21-7

Library of Congress Cataloging-in-Publication Data available.

Cover by Laura Shaw Design

For Jane and Whitney,
 my bookends

Named after the brightest star in the Northern Crown, Gemma is a nonprofit organization that helps new readers acquire English language literacy skills with relevant, engaging books, eBooks, and audiobooks. Always original, never adapted, these stories introduce adults and young adults to the life-changing power of reading.

GEMMA

Open Door

CONTENTS

CHAPTER 1
THE ACCIDENT 5

CHAPTER 2
CURIOSITY 11

CHAPTER 3
A NEW JOB 21

CHAPTER 4
GOSSIP 27

CHAPTER 5
MONEY, MONEY, MONEY 35

CHAPTER 6
A THREAT 43

CHAPTER 7
DINNER TALK 49

CHAPTER 8
TENSE TIMES 52

CHAPTER 9
A SUDDEN EVENT 55

CHAPTER 10
MS. NOSY   64

CHAPTER 11
QUESTIONS   70

CHAPTER 12
MORE MS. NOSY   77

CHAPTER 13
ANOTHER ACCIDENT   84

CHAPTER 14
A DISCOVERY   88

CHAPTER 15
DEPARTURE   92

CHAPTER 16
TAMI RETURNS   95

CHAPTER 17
WHO KILLED JULIA?   103

CAST OF CHARACTERS

Tami Tripper—A professional temporary employee and free spirit.

Julia Jackson—An old woman who owns the estate and controls her family.

Victor Jackson—Julia's son and manager of the family money.

Olivia Jackson—Victor's wife, a scientist at a local university.

Nicholas Jackson, called Nick—Julia's grandson and estate manager.

Eva Jackson—Wife of Oscar Jackson.

Kayla and Edgar Jackson—Eva's twin teens, Julia's grandchildren.

Ronnie Brooks and Tory Brooks—Household cleaner and cook, sisters.

DECEASED CHARACTERS

Henry Jackson—Prohibition-era liquor smuggler and William's father.

William Jackson—Henry's son and Julia's husband.

Oscar Jackson—Julia's son and Eva's husband.

Timothy Jackson—Julia's son and Nick's father.

CHAPTER 1

THE ACCIDENT

"Why does this kind of thing always happen to me?" Tami lay flat on her back and looked up at the night sky.

Tami was biking home from her job when she hit a deep pothole. She flew up into the air and crashed into some bushes.

Her face felt wet. Touching it, Tami's finger was sticky. "I'm bleeding!" How bad was this spill anyway? She moved her arms. Nothing broken. She tried her legs. They seemed okay. But when Tami tried to stand, her knee was *not* okay.

Tami crawled out of the bushes. She sat up, feeling dizzy. There was a lump on the back of her head. She must have hit the ground really hard.

"I need some help," she moaned. She looked for her backpack. It lay on the road, the contents scattered.

She spotted her phone. "Oh no!" It was smashed.

Tami was alone on a country road, and it was very dark. Almost midnight. She dragged herself to her feet. Her knee was swollen. Blood dripped down her leg. Maybe she could still ride her bike. But no. Her bike had a twisted front wheel and a shredded tire.

Standing on one foot in the dark night, Tami knew she was in big trouble.

She burst into tears.

"You appear to be in trouble." A voice spoke out of the dark.

Tami whipped her head around. Behind her was a man with a flashlight. He shone it slowly over her and then over her bicycle. Tami was immediately on her guard.

"I didn't hear you behind me," she said. She was not happy about the situation.

"Sorry. I did not want to frighten you."

"I'm not frightened," Tami said, although she was. She was alone on a road late at night. It was dark. She was hurt and weeping. The smart move was to run away. But how could she do that? Her knee was injured. Her bike was busted. Tami was trapped with nowhere to run.

"Can I help you? I live up the road a little way. You could lean on my shoulder and hop. It's not too far." The man's voice was pleasant.

Tami was worried, but what could she do?

"Thank you. Could we bring my bike? I need it to get to work."

"Sure. Oh, by the way, my name is Nick."

"Mine is Tami."

Nick picked up the bike with one hand. Tami grabbed his other arm. They hopped along, stopping for Tami to moan a little from the pain. In this way they finally arrived at a long, dark driveway.

"Will you wait here? I'll get our golf cart."

That sounded like a good idea to Tami. Nick returned in a few minutes. He helped Tami get seated and put the bike in the back of the cart. They motored slowly up the driveway.

As they rounded a curve, a huge house loomed in the darkness. "Oh wow," Tami gasped.

"Yes, it's quite a big old heap," laughed Nick. "Won't you come in? I could clean up your knee and give you a hot drink."

There was no way Tami was entering a strange man's house in the middle of the night.

"Thank you, but I just want to get home. Maybe you could call me a taxi."

Nick seemed disappointed, but he did not argue. The taxi arrived. Nick loaded the bike into the trunk. Tami collapsed into the back seat. "Take me to County Hospital," she told the driver.

CHAPTER 2

CURIOSITY

Tami felt a lot better. Her knee was healed. She was back at her temp job, which she hated. Tami had thought of Nick during the past two weeks. He was respectful and not at all dangerous. She owed him some thanks for helping her. Tami decided to ride her bike back to the big old house to thank him.

The day was bright and clear. Billowing clouds floated across a blue sky. There is nothing like a beautiful spring day, thought Tami. She pedaled along, humming a tune.

Tami loved to bike. She forgot her worries on her bike. Just me, living a free life, thought Tami. She sailed along, her dark, curly hair blowing in the breeze.

Tami's friends worried that she did not have a full-time job. But Tami liked variety. She liked stimulation. She liked meeting new people. She liked learning new things. She liked each day to be different. Not the same old thing. That's boring, thought Tami. I am a free spirit.

She stopped at the end of the long driveway to Nick's house. Tami opened her backpack and took out a peanut butter sandwich. Tami loved peanut butter sandwiches. Everybody loves peanut butter sandwiches, thought Tami, unless they are allergic to peanuts. Tami had two sandwiches and a sliced apple. This was her favorite lunch. She leaned against her bicycle and viewed the long driveway.

Am I making a mistake? she wondered.

Tami knew her real reason was not to thank Nick. She was curious! She wanted to see the inside of that big old house. Tami's mother used to call her "Ms. Nosy." It was not a compliment. She told Tami, "Mind your own business." Tami ignored her mother's comments and her advice. Tami was a free spirit. She went her own way and lived her own life.

Tami pedaled slowly up the driveway.

What a fabulous place! Although its outside was shabby, the house was huge. It had lots of windows, maybe twenty. Tami wondered how many bedrooms there were. Five? Seven? Ten? How about bathrooms? That was important. Did every bedroom have its own bathroom?

Tami gazed at the land around the house. It seemed to go on and on. Very quiet and very private. Rich people live here, she thought.

Tami rang the doorbell. A woman opened the door. She had a broom in her hand. "Yes?" she said.

"Hi. Is Nick home?"

The woman smiled at Tami. "You can come in and sit in the hall. I will find Nick."

Tami's mouth dropped open. Her dark eyes stared. The front hall was bigger than Tami's apartment. A glittering chandelier hung from the ceiling. A wide staircase wound upward to the floors above. Tami sat down on a bench by the entrance. The bench was covered in velvet. Tami felt out of place in this elegance. Definitely a mistake to come here. Tami turned to leave.

"Hi! Hi!" A cheery voice called. Nick ran down the staircase, a big smile on his face.

"Oh hi. I came to thank you for helping me."

"I was glad to do it. And I am glad to see you again." Nick's eyes twinkled at Tami. "Come on in."

Tami followed Nick into a large and beautiful living room. Sofas, chairs, and tables were scattered around. Many framed photographs sat on the lid of a grand piano. She walked over for a better look.

Nick laughed. "Yes, Julia Jackson has a lot of pictures in here. There are even more in her library."

"Who is Julia Jackson?" asked Tami.

"Julia Jackson is my grandmother. She owns this house and all the land around it. I am the estate manager. I live in an apartment over the garage. I have a job that I love. But I wish Grandmother would loosen the purse strings." Nick sighed. "The house needs repair. The gardens need a professional gardener. Eva loves gardening, but there is little she can do without funds."

"Eva?"

"Eva Jackson, my aunt. Eva lives here, too."

"Your grandmother, your aunt, and you live here?" asked Tami.

"Oh, that's not all," said Nick. "Eva has twin teens, Edgar and Kayla. And my uncle Victor and aunt Olivia live here, too." Another sigh. "It's a lot of family, and not everyone likes living under Julia's control."

Tami was about to ask what he meant when a figure appeared in the doorway.

"Who is your friend, Nicholas?"

A very old woman leaned on a walker. She was not smiling.

"Tami, may I introduce my grandmother, Julia Jackson?"

Tami jumped to her feet. Julia Jackson was an elegant woman in a silk dress. She wore a pearl necklace and had diamond rings on her fingers. Tami offered to shake hands, but Julia Jackson waved her away.

"Help me to sit, Nicholas," she ordered.

"Grandmother, you should not move around the house by yourself," Nick scolded with a smile.

"Nicholas, you may be in charge of this estate, but I am the owner. Do not think you can scold me or treat me like an invalid. There are other men who would like your job *and* your nice apartment."

I guess I know who's the boss around here, thought Tami.

Julia Jackson sat down and pushed the walker out of sight. She clearly hated it. "Again I ask, who is your friend, Nicholas?"

"Tami is the woman who fell off her

bicycle a few weeks ago. That's all I can tell you."

"Then perhaps the young woman can answer my question, as you are unable to do so."

Tami smiled. "My name is Tamina Tripper, but everyone calls me Tami. I work at the computer company. One lovely night, I decided to ride home on a quiet road. My bike hit a pothole, and I fell off, hurting my knee. Nick called a taxi for me. I thought I should come back to thank him."

"Very appropriate," agreed the old lady. "Do you like working at night?"

"Not particularly," said Tami. "It is a temp job."

"A temp job?" repeated Nick. "You don't have a full-time job?"

Why are people always so surprised? thought Tami.

"Full-time jobs don't match my personality," she explained. "I like variety. I like change. I like meeting new people. I like discovering new places. I am a *professional temporary employee*. I have a lot of skills that I've learned from my many jobs," Tami added proudly.

Julia Jackson eyed Tami with interest. "I like your independent spirit, Tamina. You are making your own way, not sponging off other people." Julia frowned. Nick looked embarrassed.

Julia's remark surprised Tami. Was Julia referring to her own relatives? Tami was more and more curious about the house and the people in it.

CHAPTER 3

A NEW JOB

"You may have noticed my photographs." Julia Jackson waved her hand toward the piano. "There are even more in the library. I need someone to organize them. Are you interested?"

Tami was thrilled. If she accepted, she could leave that horrible night job. And she would be able to satisfy her curiosity.

"Thank you, Mrs. Jackson. I would love to organize your photographs. I can begin whenever you wish."

"What a great idea." Nick smiled. He was obviously pleased.

"I am hiring Tamina to work for me.

I am not hiring Tamina so you can look at a pretty face." Julia turned to Tami. "You start tomorrow. I will see you in the morning at ten. Be on time." Shoving her walker in front of her, Julia Jackson left the room.

Tami turned to Nick. "I would like to do a good job for your grandmother. Do you have any advice for me?"

"Why don't you come over to my apartment for some coffee? I can give you a better picture of how this household works," said Nick.

Tami and Nick walked to his apartment over the old garage. It was huge. It had big windows. It had a sunny bedroom. The kitchen sparkled. Nick has a really good deal here, thought Tami.

"Tell me about Julia Jackson."

"Well," began Nick. "Julia is about eighty-five years old. Nobody really knows her age, because she won't tell. She will not admit that she is getting old and that her body is breaking down. She has a number of health issues that she will not discuss. For instance, she takes insulin for diabetes and has serious allergies."

"Who else lives here?"

"Julia had three sons—Victor, Oscar, and Timothy. Only Uncle Victor is still alive. He is about sixty, and he runs the family company. Julia belittles and criticizes Victor." Nick was no longer smiling.

"Victor's wife, Olivia, is a scientist at the local university. Her field is poisonous plants. Her dream is to do research in Costa Rica. But Victor is trapped working for Julia, so Olivia is stuck here. My aunt Eva is Oscar's widow. After Oscar died, Eva came here with her twins, Edgar and Kayla. And then there is me. I am Timothy's son. I have lived here since my parents died when I was twelve. That's the family. In this house, my grandmother gets her own way. Everyone does what Julia wants. This is a house of unhappy people. Are you sure you want the job?"

When Tami got home that evening, she recalled Nick's words. *This is a house of unhappy people.* Julia Jackson was not a warm, loving woman. The Jackson family did not seem to care about each other.

Tami grew up with just her mom. She missed their talks and the fun they had together. Tami's mom gave Tami a bicycle when she was nine years old. Tami named the bike Ruby, because it was a bright ruby red. Now Tami always rode a red bike. And all of Tami's bikes were named Ruby to remember her mom.

Tami's mom loved life. Even as she battled cancer, Tami's mom remained positive. "I don't worry about you, Tami," said her mom. "Tamina means 'strong,' and you are strong like your name. I know you will be okay." Tami missed her mom. Tami was alone, but she grew up with a lot of love. She had a happy outlook on life, just like her mom. Tami felt sorry for the Jacksons.

CHAPTER 4

GOSSIP

The next morning, Tami was led into the library. Julia Jackson sat in a chair covered in gold fabric. She wore another elegant gown. Next to her was a small table with a coffeepot and a cup and saucer. She had a lace napkin on her lap. No chipped mugs and paper napkins for Julia Jackson, thought Tami.

"Where should I begin?" Tami's eyes scanned the room. She noticed a large framed portrait of a couple in wedding clothes. "Is this you?" she asked Julia. "What a beautiful satin gown. And your lace veil is so delicate. You were a beautiful bride, Mrs. Jackson."

"Yes, I was," agreed Julia Jackson. "My husband, William, was lucky to marry me. I had plenty of offers. Plenty," she added.

"Why don't I start with photographs of your wedding? They will be easy to identify."

"An excellent idea. I will be back at the end of the day to review your work." Pushing her walker, Julia Jackson departed. She closed the library door behind her.

Tami got to work. She sat on the floor and sorted through a box of photographs. Tami was humming quietly to herself when the door opened two hours later.

A woman poked her head into the room. She was the cleaner who let Tami into the house. "Hi, I'm Ronnie Brooks. Would you like to come to the kitchen for lunch?"

Tami was hungry. "I'd love to come. I'll bring my lunch." Tami held up a plastic bag with her limp peanut butter sandwich.

"Leave that in your backpack. Julia is allergic to peanuts. And bee stings," Ronnie added. "Anyway, I think you will enjoy our food a lot more. Follow me."

Standing at a large stove was a woman who looked a lot like Ronnie. "Meet my sister, Tory. Tory cooks, and I clean."

"Sometimes you cook, and I clean," remarked Tory with a laugh.

"It's true that my grilled cheese

sandwiches are better than yours," teased Ronnie.

Tami was glad to meet these two lively sisters. I bet they know a lot about what goes on in this house, she thought.

Tory set bowls of French onion soup with hot bubbling cheese on the kitchen table. Next came a green salad with sweet orange slices. "Dig in!" she ordered.

After lunch, Tami sat back in her chair and gazed at the sisters. "Do you live here, too?"

"No way!" answered Ronnie. "We bike in from the village every day. Then we go home at night after serving dinner."

"We would never, never live here," added Tory. "This family is so unhappy.

Even my delicious food can't sweeten their moods."

"But we get to hear some juicy tidbits of information." Ronnie grinned.

"Like what?"

"Like the fact that Olivia was offered space in a science lab in Costa Rica. She could finally study poisonous plants in the wild," said Tory.

"I just happened to overhear them," Ronnie added. "Olivia said, 'Victor, when are you going to grow up and stand on your own two feet? This place is a prison!' Then Victor said, 'I'll get us out of here, one way or another.'"

"They were angry and frustrated," said Tory. "And I don't blame them."

"Why are they all living under one

roof?" asked Tami. "It's like something out of an old movie."

"Victor and Olivia live here because Victor manages the family's money. Julia insists that he do it from the house. Eva is stuck here with the twins. She is expected to cater to Julia's whims. And Nick lives in the apartment over the old garage. Julia likes controlling the lives of her family," explained Ronnie.

Biking home on Ruby, Tami reviewed her first day at the Jackson house. She enjoyed sorting through the photographs. And Ms. Nosy was entertained by gossip from Ronnie and Tory. This job will be very interesting, she thought.

When Tami arrived home, there was a delivery box on her doorstep. Tami was excited. Tami loved music, but she had never learned to play an instrument. She had talked to the owner of the local music store. He had shown her a beautiful clarinet and said it was perfect for a beginner like Tami.

Tami opened the box and gazed with delight at her clarinet. It was bright, shiny, and ruby red—Tami's favorite color. Tami carefully fitted the pieces together. She put her lips over the mouth piece and tooted. It was so much fun!

Tami had a book called *How to Play the Clarinet*. She learned "Row, Row, Row Your Boat" by bedtime. She decided to practice every night. She placed her new red clarinet on the table next to her bed. She would see it first thing in the morning. Tami was in love!

CHAPTER 5

MONEY, MONEY, MONEY

Over the next few weeks Tami sorted photographs in Julia Jackson's library. Different family members drifted in and out of the room. They want to check me out, thought Tami with amusement. Nick often sat and chatted while Tami sorted.

"What does an estate manager do?" she asked Nick.

"I oversee the house and grounds. I am responsible for repairs to all the buildings. I supervise Ronnie and Tory. I also manage the budget."

"It sounds like a big job. So why are

you sitting around this room watching me work instead?"

"I give Grandmother a list of repairs and how much they will cost. She looks at the list and says, 'No.' Julia sits on a pile of money, but she lets this place go to ruin." Nick's face was flushed with anger.

"Why don't you get a job somewhere else?"

"Maybe I like seeing you," Nick suggested.

"That's no excuse," Tami said.

One afternoon, a pale, thin woman wandered in.

"Have you seen my children?"

This must be Eva Jackson, thought Tami.

"No, I haven't."

"Are you Tami?" Eva's voice was very soft and low.

"Yes. I'm glad to meet you. Your garden is lovely."

"Oh thank you! If only I was allowed to do more! This estate could be really beautiful. It is my dream to restore and expand the gardens." Eva was silent for a moment. "It will happen one day. I want it so much . . ." Eva's voice trailed off, and she wandered out of the library.

Eva Jackson is like a faded flower herself, thought Tami. How sad.

Two teens poked their heads in shortly after. "Is our mother in here?"

"She was here a few minutes ago.

I think she's looking for you in the garden."

"Good. Let's stay here so she won't find us," said the girl.

"Are you Nick's girlfriend?" The boy asked.

"No I am not," responded Tami. "I am here on a job. You two must be Edgar and Kayla."

"Obviously," snorted Kayla. She looked at Tami's photo piles. "You don't seem to be getting much done. I hope my grandmother is not paying you a lot of money."

"Of course Grandmother isn't paying Tami well. Grandmother is a tightwad. She is an old witch," added Edgar.

"What your grandmother pays me

is none of your business. And it is not polite to criticize your family to a total stranger."

"Why not?" said Kayla. "The old witch won't give us any money. She's rich and could give us lots, but she won't! She's not even a real Jackson. She just married a Jackson. Probably for his money, since she got it all when he died. We really hate her, don't we Edgar? If she gave me money, I could go to California to be a movie star. But Grandmother just sneers at me and calls me a no-talent teenager!"

"Everybody in this house hates Grandmother," said Edgar. "We wait and wait for her to die. I wish she would hurry up!"

Tami was shocked. These teens did not know how to keep their mouths shut.

"Let's go," said Kayla. "This person is no fun." She glared at Tami.

"I need my sketchbook," said Edgar.

"You and your old insects! How boring. What's the point of drawing them all day?"

"Insects are beautiful. I plan to be a nature illustrator. I'm going to publish a book. I'll be more famous than you," Edgar said to Kayla. "I want to go to Costa Rica with Aunt Olivia."

"Don't hold your breath. Grandmother will never let Uncle Victor and Aunt Olivia out of her clutches. And Mother is hopeless with money, so she is no help to us, " Kayla added viciously.

The twins left the library. Money, money, money, thought Tami. It's all anyone cares about in this house. Including Nick.

Tami could not wait to get home that night. She wanted to practice her new clarinet. It was so much fun. And she was tired of listening to the Jacksons complain about money. Money isn't everything, she said to herself. Tami and her mom never had much money, but they were happy.

After her mom died, Tami moved to an apartment over a store. The store sold Native American baskets made out of sweetgrass. Tami bought two. Tami's great-great-grandmother was Native

American, so a tiny part of Tami was Native American. The baskets reminded Tami of her mom.

Tami climbed the stairs to her apartment. My teeny-tiny home, she thought. Only three rooms. The living room was Tami's favorite room. It was small with tall windows that looked out on the street below. Shelves held Tami's many books. There was a sofa and a chair and a plant. Her mom's paintings hung on one wall. Best of all, the walls were painted red. Tami put a lot of love into her cozy home. A fancy house does not mean a happy home, she thought to herself. Tami liked her life just the way it was.

CHAPTER 6

A THREAT

The weeks passed. In the library, Tami hummed as she sorted photographs. One afternoon she heard arguing in the next room.

"Mother, no!" Victor's voice was loud.

"I'll do what I want, Victor."

"Mother, please don't do this."

"Remember, Victor, the business and the estate belong to me. No one can stop me if I want to sell them. If I want to go live in a hotel, I can. I am tired of being surrounded by this bloodsucking family."

"Mother, are you serious about this? Or is it just a threat?"

"No, it is not just a threat, Victor. Why should I keep this house? I don't care about it anymore."

"But we all live here, too. Where would we go?"

"That is your problem. Figure it out yourselves. I am done with you." And with slow steps, Julia Jackson left the room.

Tami could not believe her ears. She heard the rest of the family rush into the room.

"Victor! What is going on?" Olivia demanded.

"I heard yelling," said Eva.

The twins burst in. "What is it? What is it?"

"I am here, too," Nick said.

"Mother threatened to sell everything, take the money, and live in a hotel!" Victor was furious.

"She's lost her mind," whispered Eva. "The twins and I would have nowhere to live. And what about the garden? I can't leave the garden!"

"Does that mean there won't be any money for us when she dies? I need to get to California," said Kayla.

"And I need to go to Costa Rica with Aunt Olivia and Uncle Victor," added Edgar.

"No one is going to Costa Rica without the money to pay for it," said Olivia bitterly. "Julia has shattered my dreams."

"My plans for this estate will never happen now," Nick added.

Silence fell.

"Why do we wait and wait for Julia to die if she isn't going to do it?" Eva's voice was low but very, very clear.

"Yes, she needs to hurry up," Kayla added.

Tami remembered she was eavesdropping. Grabbing her jacket and backpack, she slipped quietly out of the house.

At home, Tami got out her clarinet. She could play "Jingle Bells" and "Happy Birthday." Now she practiced "Ode to Joy." It was a famous piece of music by Beethoven. Tami was happy to be finished with children's songs.

As she tooted her clarinet, Tami recalled the conversation she heard. She did not think Julia Jackson was going to die anytime soon. Julia was careful about her health. Eva was responsible for Julia's nightly insulin injections. Tory kept peanuts at a safe distance. No flowers came in from the garden to keep out bees. Julia Jackson was strong and capable. She was very much in charge of her household and her family. Now Julia's threat put the Jacksons' dreams in danger. What would happen? wondered Tami.

Nick resented Julia's refusal to improve the estate.

Eva feared she would lose the garden.

Olivia was desperate to get to Costa Rica.

Victor's anger at his mother was ready to boil over.

And Tami had been shocked by the poison in Kayla's and Edgar's voices. Those two are greedy and sly, she thought.

It was a bad situation.

CHAPTER 7

DINNER TALK

Tami went straight to the kitchen the next day.

"Wait until you hear about last night!" Tory handed her a cup of coffee.

"We served dinner as usual," Ronnie began.

"A beautiful, flaky fish with tender asparagus and tiny roasted potatoes," said Tory.

"No one spoke a word during the meal. It was creepy," said Ronnie. "When we served dessert, Mrs. Jackson left the room."

"An apple tart," said Tory.

"We usually leave then, but last night

we decided to linger right outside the dining room door," said Ronnie. "We heard everything."

Tory explained. "Olivia said, 'Everyone at this table will be penniless and homeless if Julia follows through on her threat. And you, Victor. When are you going to take charge of anything? Spineless, that's you.'

"'Don't be so quick to criticize me, Olivia. There are ways around every situation.'

"Eva began to weep. 'That's right, Mother,' hissed Kayla. 'Cry. Very effective. Crying always solves problems.'

"'We're all pathetic,' Edgar said. 'Mother lets Grandmother boss her around. Uncle Victor and Aunt Olivia dream about Costa Rica. Kayla longs for stardom. I want to publish my drawings. And Nick cannot wait to turn the estate into a showplace. We all want that old woman dead.'

"'With Mother's medical issues, it's a miracle she hasn't died already,' murmured Victor.

"'True,' added Nick. 'Insulin shock, a bee sting, or one of Tami's peanut butter sandwiches would do the trick.'"

"What happened then?" asked Tami.

Tory and Ronnie laughed. "They ate the apple tart!"

CHAPTER 8

TENSE TIMES

The atmosphere was tense in the days following Julia's threat. Tami often heard family members talking among themselves.

Eva panicked. She talked to Nick. "I've been quiet. I've held my tongue every time that woman criticized or made fun of me. I haven't complained once during all these years. The garden has been my joy. Now she is taking it from me. I need the garden. I deserve the garden. I can't leave, and I won't leave!"

"It would be hard for me, too," said Nick. "You are not the only one with a dream." He stormed out of the house and jumped into the golf cart. He raced it around and around the grounds of the estate trying to blow off steam.

Olivia quarreled with Victor. "The lab in Costa Rica recognizes the important work that I do. I am entitled to realize my ambitions. I plan to be a world expert on poisonous plants. Your mother can't keep me from my destiny. I will find a way to get to Costa Rica!"

"Olivia, what about me? I would have to find a job. Who will hire a sixty-year-old man whose only job was working for his mother? And who fired him!"

Kayla screamed and cried in her room and threw her possessions at the walls.

Not a sound escaped Edgar's room. He was plunged in misery.

The lives of six people would be in turmoil if Julia Jackson made good on her threat to sell everything and take the money.

CHAPTER 9

A SUDDEN EVENT

Two days later, Ronnie ran out of the kitchen door screaming. Tami was parking Ruby in the driveway.

"She's dead! When I brought her morning tray, she was lying half in and half out of her bed. Dead, dead, dead!" Ronnie pulled Tami into the kitchen.

Tory said, "The doctor thinks it was a heart attack."

"Really?" asked Tami. "I didn't know she had anything wrong with her heart."

"The doctor said any old person's heart can give out without warning."

"I suppose so," murmured Tami.

In the library, Tami gazed at the

boxes of photos. She might lose her job today. Julia Jackson was irritable and found fault. She criticized Tami's hair, clothing, and her lifestyle. She insisted on calling her Tamina instead of Tami. But Tami enjoyed this job. She would be sorry to lose it.

The twins laughed in the next room.

"Now I can leave this prison and go to Hollywood." It was Kayla's voice. "Edgar, soon you will tell people that your sister is a movie star."

"You wish," sneered Edgar. "Maybe it will be the other way around. Maybe I will win an award for my books."

"Oh, insects are so boring. But your illustrations are pretty decent," Kayla admitted.

"I told you to keep out of my room."

"I only took a peek at your stupid drawings."

Tami had seen Edgar in the gardens with his sketchbook, drawing insects and recording their behavior. Those twin teenagers are a cold-blooded pair, thought Tami. They don't care about anyone.

People came and went. The coroner and the doctor. The morticians with their van. The family's lawyer. Ronnie and Tory rushed around. Telephone calls were made. Everyone was busy. Not a single person seemed sad.

Nick and Victor argued with the doctor. "Why is there an autopsy?" demanded Victor.

"Yes," added Nick. "An eighty-five-year-old woman dies in her sleep. It happens every day."

"It's the law," answered the doctor. "Sudden death requires an autopsy. Please don't let it concern you. It is routine."

Nick came into the library at the end of the day. He threw himself into a chair. "Thank goodness that part is over. Grandmother's body has gone to the coroner's office. The lawyer will read us the will in a few hours. Then everyone can make plans."

"Is the will a secret?" asked Tami.

"No, we know most of it. The business is shared between Uncle Victor and Aunt Eva. Grandmother left me the house and land. Of course, Edgar and Kayla hope to inherit some money."

"The lives of everyone in this household are suddenly better," commented Tami.

"They sure are. Blue skies ahead for all of us."

"Except for me. I'm out of a job." Tami pointed to the photographs.

"Maybe not," smiled Nick. "Maybe I have some ideas that include you."

Tami did not ask what he meant. She did not want to start an uncomfortable conversation.

The lawyer read Julia's will late that afternoon. Victor, Eva, and Nick received what was expected. Edgar and Kayla each received $100,000, but not until they were twenty-five years old. At first the teens were angry. But they learned Eva would give them large allowances.

Ronnie and Tory gasped when they learned that Julia Jackson had left them each $5000, "in thanks for their delicious food and sparkling rooms."

Tami joined them in the kitchen afterward.

"I take back all the mean things I said about her," Tory said.

"Me too," agreed Ronnie. "I can't believe she left us money! She was such a tightwad when she was alive."

"Didn't she pay you well?" Tami's wages were very fair.

"Oh, she paid us the usual rate. It's not really the money, it's that she complimented us. She never once mentioned our 'delicious food and sparkling rooms'!"

"What do you think the Jacksons will do now that Julia Jackson is dead?"

"The company will be sold. It is worth many millions. Then Victor and Olivia will go to Costa Rica. Olivia will study poisonous plants, and Victor will play golf," said Ronnie.

Tory said, "Nick and Eva have plans for the estate. Kayla will move to Hollywood to be a star. She hasn't got any talent, but she will land on her feet. People like Kayla always do."

"What about Edgar?"

"Edgar is like Kayla, very ambitious. His plans for an illustrated book of insects are impressive. Something could come of it."

Biking home on Ruby, Tami did not notice the warm afternoon. Wasn't it odd that Julia Jackson died so soon after her threat? Tami shivered. The timing was curious. Tami heard her mother's voice. *Mind your own business, Ms. Nosy.*

Tami opened the computer on her kitchen table. She searched the internet. Tami learned about Nick's great-grandfather, Henry Jackson. He was a bootlegger during the 1920s when liquor was illegal in the United States. As a young man, Henry Jackson smuggled liquor in from Canada. Henry Jackson soon made a lot of money. His son William, Julia's husband, invested the money and became very rich. When William died, Julia inherited everything.

Now Julia Jackson was dead, and her children and grandchildren had all the money. But what killed her?

CHAPTER 10

MS. NOSY

The following day Tami made lists of photographs. Maybe someone wanted them, but she doubted it.

Nick joined her in the library.

"What you will do with the estate?" asked Tami. "Will you sell it?"

"No. I am turning it into a small exclusive hotel, as I always wanted to do. The bedrooms will be suites for hotel guests. The living room, library, dining room, and kitchen can be easily remodeled." There was excitement in Nick's voice.

"What about the gardens and grounds?"

"It's all arranged. Eva will design the grounds. She can't wait to get started. She wants a swimming pool and tennis courts. Ronnie and Tory will stay, too. They will have a small staff to help them." Nick had clearly planned this for years.

Tami continued to be shocked at the Jackson family's behavior. No one seemed sad or sorry about Julia's death. No one discussed funeral arrangements. The family acted like prisoners who had been freed. Had life here been that bad? Yes, Julia had not been a loveable person. But she had provided a home, employment, and financial support for six family members. Was no one grateful?

Tami brooded about the timing of Julia's death. Only two days after her threat! Only two days after that dinner conversation! Tami could not let it go. Ms. Nosy had to know more.

That afternoon Tami visited Julia's bedroom. It looked like a hotel room. Impersonal. Clean. A window was open. Tami poked her head out. Just below the windowsill, Eva's favorite June roses were in bloom, their red colors glowing in the afternoon sun. Their scent filled the air, outside and inside. Bees flew from flower to flower. Tami saw Eva working in the garden. Edgar sat sketching on the ground. The open window added to the room's strangeness. Julia's bedroom windows were always closed.

Tami turned back to the room. The bedside table was bare. Gone were the details of Julia Jackson's everyday life—a glass of water, insulin injections, a lipstick and mirror, a box of tissues, and the usual plate of Tory's yummy brownies. All that remained was a lamp.

Tami wondered where Julia's EpiPen was. The EpiPen had a needle with medication that could save Julia's life during an allergic reaction. It was always on her bedside table.

Tami looked under the bed. She opened the closet. She inspected the bathroom. It was the same everywhere. Clean and impersonal. Only the portrait of Julia that hung on the wall remained. The portrait was large and set in a gold frame. In it, Julia was seated in a gold chair. She looked about forty years old.

Behind the chair stood a handsome man, Julia's husband William. Julia's three sons completed the picture—Victor, Oscar, and Timothy. Julia looked happy.

Victor came quietly into the room. "My father died not long after that was painted. Then my brothers Oscar and Timothy both died." He sighed. "My mother became an angry, disappointed woman." He gazed around. "Now that woman is dead, taking her bitterness with her. Her family can breathe freely again. It's been a long wait. For some of us maybe a little too long."

🚲

That night, as Tami played her ruby-red clarinet, she suddenly stopped. Tami's mind was not on the music. Putting down her clarinet, Tami went back to the internet. Ms. Nosy was curious about allergies.

CHAPTER 11

QUESTIONS

The family lawyer arranged a funeral. At the reception, Tami approached Julia's doctor.

"Excuse me, can you tell me how Mrs. Jackson died?"

"She died of heart failure."

"What causes heart failure?"

"It's usually caused by heart disease."

"Did Mrs. Jackson have heart disease?"

"No, she didn't." The doctor frowned.

"Can shock cause heart failure?" Tami asked.

"Insulin shock? Eva was very careful with Julia's injections for diabetes."

"What about another kind of shock?" Tami persisted.

"What other kind?" The doctor was losing patience.

"Mrs. Jackson had serious allergies."

"Yes, she did. But they were under control, too. Julia was eighty-five. She just died of old age." The doctor walked away. A few minutes later he was deep in conversation with Victor.

Tami helped Tory and Ronnie clean up after the reception. "Ronnie, did you notice anything odd on the day that Julia died?"

"You mean besides Julia's dead body? That was enough. My screaming brought the entire family."

"But later, when you cleaned her room. How about then?"

"Like what?"

"Was a window open?"

"I don't think so. Anyway, the windows were always closed to keep the bees out."

"What about her bedside table?"

"It was knocked over. She must have done it herself. Her body was lying half on the bed and half off of it."

"Was the plate of brownies knocked over? What about the EpiPen?"

"The brownies were scattered all over. Later, I found the EpiPen under the bed. It must have rolled under there."

"What's this all about, Tami?" asked Tory.

"Julia died of heart failure, right? But she didn't have heart disease. So what made her heart stop? She was healthy and strong. She had diabetes, but Eva was careful about the insulin injections."

"Yes," Ronnie agreed.

"What about her allergies? You told me that a teaspoon of peanut butter could kill Julia. Or a bee sting."

"Wait a minute, Tami. There is no peanut butter in this kitchen. I was very, very careful." Tory was annoyed.

"That window above the climbing roses was never open," added Ronnie. "Never."

"But there was peanut butter in this house. My peanut butter sandwich. I keep one in my backpack. And that window only needed to be opened a crack for a bee to fly in. Anyone could have opened it during the night and closed it in the morning's confusion."

"Are you trying to tell us something, Tami?" asked Tory.

"What if a bee stung Julia? Or there was a tiny amount of peanut butter in the brownies? Julia could have died of shock."

"Shock! You mean an allergic reaction?"

"Yes, Julia would not be able to breathe. Her blood pressure would drop. I read about it on the internet. Without her EpiPen to stop the reaction, she would die. And her EpiPen was under her bed."

The sisters exchanged a look.

"I'm just saying it's possible. Definitely possible," insisted Tami.

Tami's mom said that Tami's nose was always either in a book or in somebody else's business. That night Tami's nose was in both places. She scanned her floor-to-ceiling shelves of books. Maybe one of them would help her solve the mystery of Julia Jackson's death. She found one of her favorite books, *Murderers and Their Personalities*. One section of the book was underlined.

"Murderers have a cold-blooded attitude toward others. They believe they deserve whatever they want. They think rules don't apply to them. Disappointment, frustration, anger, greed, or pride simmer below the surface. If they boil over, murder can happen."

Tami closed the book and stared into space. A cold-blooded attitude.

Anger. Greed. Frustration. Those words described more than one Jackson family member. Was one of them a murderer?

CHAPTER 12

MORE MS. NOSY

The next day, Tami found herself in an empty house. The family was meeting with their lawyer. Tory and Ronnie were in town shopping for supplies. Tami was alone.

She went to the top of the house and worked her way down. She started with the adults. In their bedrooms she opened desks, read papers, inspected dresser drawers, and peered over the tops of cabinets. She searched the pockets of their clothes.

Tami discovered the secret plans of each adult. Victor had information about how much the company was worth. Olivia had written a letter to the research lab in Costa Rica. Quiet Eva had designed the grounds of the estate.

Tami tackled the twins' rooms next. Edgar's room was extremely tidy. His paintings lay on a long table. Tami examined a wasp, a ladybug, and a grasshopper. Each painting showed tiny details. There were notes about each insect. Edgar is a naturalist, thought Tami. No wonder he wants to go to Costa Rica.

Kayla's room was the opposite. Clothes flung everywhere. The walls were plastered with photos of herself. She had an enormous makeup collection and a wig collection. On a long shelf were books of plays and musicals. *Romeo and Juliet. The Lion King. West Side Story.* Kayla had over one hundred plays. Maybe Kayla would end up a star. Who knew?

Tami's next stop was Nick's apartment over the garage. She had been there a few times. She turned over papers and poked around closets. Tami found drawings for a hotel in a hidden folder. Nick had planned well ahead of Julia's death, too.

As she walked down the stairs to the yard below, she heard footsteps. Quickly, Tami scampered back up the stairs just as Nick appeared in the apartment's doorway.

"Tami! What are you doing here?" Nick's eyes scanned the room. "Did you want something from my apartment?"

"Oh, I'm sorry to startle you. I need more paper, and I thought you would have some. And you did." Tami held up a stack of paper.

"That's okay. I just wish you would ask before dropping by when I'm not here."

Tami apologized again. She ran down the stairs and across the garden to the house. Whew! She had grabbed the paper just in time.

At the end of the day, Tami was ready to go home and think about her discoveries. She was getting onto Ruby when she heard voices in the garden nearby.

"Victor, someone has been nosing around. My papers have been disturbed. And Eva says her desk drawers were open."

"Maybe it was Ronnie. She cleans the rooms."

"I asked her. She and Tory were shopping. The only person in the house was Tami."

"Nick discovered Tami alone in his apartment," said Victor.

"Maybe Tami's job here should come to an end," muttered Olivia. "After all, we don't really know anything about her."

Hearing that conversation helped Tami decide what to do. Hopping on her bike she pedaled down the long driveway. She turned in a different direction instead of heading home. She was seated in the sheriff's office minutes later.

"I hear what you're saying, Tami, but it sounds so far-fetched. Mrs. Jackson was eighty-five. Why shouldn't her heart just give out?"

"Mrs. Jackson was a strong woman," insisted Tami. "She did not have heart disease. But she did have two allergies—peanuts and bee stings. That entire family wanted her to die. Maybe someone decided to speed things up. Maybe someone put peanut butter in her food."

"Tami, be sensible. You are imagining things. The doctor and coroner both agree on the cause of death."

"It's the timing, Sheriff. Mrs. Jackson died immediately after her threat to the family. It's so suspicious! I can't stop thinking about it."

"Tami, now I understand why your mom called you Ms. Nosy. Mrs. Jackson died in her sleep. Please just get back on your bike and go home."

Tami stomped out of the sheriff's office and slammed the door. She knew something bad happened at the Jackson house, but no one was listening to her.

CHAPTER 13

ANOTHER ACCIDENT

Tami was in the library humming a new clarinet piece when Nick stuck his head in. "Tami, will you please join us in the living room?"

The entire Jackson family had gathered. No one was smiling.

"Tami, we were surprised to get a phone call from the sheriff this morning. He asked about Julia's allergies. Apparently, you visited him yesterday." It was Victor speaking.

Then Nick spoke. "Tami, we're disappointed that you did that. Julia is dead. The coroner issued a death certificate.

The family should be left in peace to mourn our mother and grandmother."

"I just wondered what caused her heart attack," protested Tami.

"Julia died of old age. It happens every day," said Victor. "The subject is closed. Let's finish the estate business and move on with our lives."

The family filed out of the room talking among themselves.

Well, they told me off, thought Tami. And I'm not buying that bit about mourning Julia's death. What hypocrites!

It was a relief to leave the Jackson house that evening. The family no longer wanted her around. Maybe it is time for Ms. Nosy to leave this job, Tami wondered. She did not know what to do. Tami pedaled home deep in thought. Stop brooding, she told herself. It is a lovely evening. Enjoy your ride home. She rode faster and faster.

Tami always coasted her bike down the steep hill that led to her home. At the bottom of the hill was an intersection with traffic lights. When Tami started down the hill, the light was green. But the light turned red just as she reached the bottom. Tami squeezed her bike's hand brakes hard, but nothing happened. Something was wrong with her brakes! Tami was out of control. Her bike raced wildly through the red light. Cars honked their horns. Voices screamed "Watch out!" Tami crashed into a fence and tumbled off.

People came running. "Are you hurt? Why didn't you stop? You could have been killed. That car barely missed you!"

Tami stood up. "I do not understand. I keep my bike in good shape." She examined her bicycle. The front brakes were bent. How had that happened? When she hit the fence? Or . . .? Tami recalled the conversation between Victor and Olivia. *Maybe Tami's job here should come to an end.*

CHAPTER 14

A DISCOVERY

In a few weeks everything changed. The company was sold. Victor, Olivia, and Edgar left for Costa Rica. Kayla was on her way to California. Nick talked to architects and contractors. Eva's garden plans were spread around the living room. The Jacksons' long wait for Julia's death was over.

Tami finished organizing Julia Jackson's photographs. There were five boxes. Each box was labeled. Julia's Childhood. Julia & William's Wedding. Julia's Sons. Special Occasions. Miscellaneous. Tami had a photo list for each box typed in her laptop computer. Only one task was left. To print the lists and place them inside the boxes.

Tami picked up her laptop and went to the estate office. This was a room near the kitchen where Victor and Nick worked. The room had desks with computers and telephones. There were shelves with books about estate management, investing money, and plants. The printer was on top of a filing cabinet.

Tami loaded paper into the printer and pressed start. Tami needed to print twenty pages. While she waited, Tami looked around. She opened desk drawers and filing cabinets. Tami knew her mother would say, "Mind you own business, Ms. Nosy." Tami opened one of the gardening books. A piece of paper fell onto the floor. Tami glanced at the paper and gasped. It was an internet article titled "Allergies and Death." Tami read it carefully.

"Many deaths from allergic reactions do not leave any trace. This is because the death is from shock caused by the reaction, not the allergy."

Tami sat down suddenly. She was right after all. One of the Jacksons was a murderer. But who?

Was it Kayla or Edgar with their cold-blooded attitudes? Olivia, who believed she should have whatever she wanted? Victor, whose pride had been destroyed by his mother? Quiet Eva, obsessed with her garden? Or Nick? Nick, who was finally building his dream hotel.

Tami stared at the article in her hand. There was no way to find out who printed the article or when. But Tami had a feeling in her bones.

Tami pictured someone creeping into Julia's dark bedroom holding a jar. An angry bee was in the jar. The lid was opened. The bee found Julia's bare arm. Its stinger plunged into Julia's flesh and the bee died. The murderer left the room with the dead bee in the jar. Julia gasped for breath. She knocked over her bedside table, grabbing for the EpiPen. But Julia would never find her EpiPen. It had been kicked under the bed.

Tami believed she knew who murdered Julia Jackson. But the internet article was not proof.

CHAPTER 15

DEPARTURE

"It's time for me to go," Tami said to Nick.

"I thought you would stay! We need help with the hotel. And I hoped our friendship would get closer. Please stay." Nick was shocked by Tami's decision. "You would have a full-time job," he added.

Tami gave Nick a smile.

"Have you forgotten what I told you the very first day? I am a *temporary* employee. Full-time jobs are not for me. A free spirit follows her own path."

Nick said, "Are you sure you won't stay? You could write a history of the

Jacksons and use the photos as illustrations. Doesn't that sound like fun?" Nick's face was hopeful.

Nick's offer was tempting, but Tami knew it was time to go. "Let's part friends," she said to Nick. Tami climbed onto Ruby and pedaled slowly away. At the end of the long driveway, she looked back at the house. She remembered her first view of it—an enormous, shabby mansion with twenty windows. She had been so curious!

Tami had worked many jobs: in computer labs, in hospitals, in schools, in offices, in magazines, hotels, and restaurants. Tami could figure out what made people tick because she easily made friends.

But Tami's incurable curiosity led to

a very different outcome with the Jacksons. Maybe even a dangerous one. The failure of her bicycle brakes was never explained. It was time to move on.

Home at last, Tami took the article out of her backpack and put it in an envelope. On a separate paper Tami wrote the name of the murderer. She folded it and added it to the envelope. She sealed the envelope. Tami went to her bookshelves. She opened *Murderers and Their Personalities* and slipped the envelope inside. It is important to save every clue, thought Tami. You never know what the future will bring.

CHAPTER 16

TAMI RETURNS

Tami rode Ruby to a newsstand early one morning. She pulled up in front of Sam's News and hopped off her bike.

"Hi Sam," said Tami. "I want to learn bike repair. Do you have a magazine that will help me?"

"How about this one?" Sam held up a magazine called *Fix It Yourself*. It had a picture of a broken bicycle on the cover.

"Looks perfect," said Tami. A newspaper headline caught her eye. "STRANGE DEATH STILL A MYSTERY!" Tami's eyes widened.

"I'll take this newspaper, too." Tami's voice trembled with excitement.

She raced home and ran up the stairs to her apartment. She opened the newspaper and read the article three times. Tami sat at her kitchen table and thought. Then Tami sent an international email.

Tami waited three hours for a response. When it came, she stuffed *Murderers and Their Personalities* into her backpack, ran back down the stairs, and jumped onto Ruby.

Tami was at the driveway leading to the Jackson home in an hour. She pedaled slowly up to the house. It felt strange to be back. One year had passed. Tami saw many changes. The gardens bloomed with flowers. The house had a new coat of paint. Tami read the sign by the entrance: *WELCOME TO THE JACKSON INN.* How will they react to my news? Tami wondered.

The front door flew open. Ronnie ran out and hugged Tami. "I saw you through the window! Tory, Nick, Eva," Ronnie called. "Tami is here!"

"We missed you," said Tory, also hugging Tami.

Eva smiled gently. "It is so nice to see you again."

Nick grinned. "I agree! Have you come to see the changes we made?"

"Of course, I want to see everything," said Tami. "But I am here about something else. Something important. Something you may not want to hear."

"Let's go into the library," suggested Nick.

When Eva, Tory, Ronnie, and Nick were seated, Tami spoke.

"One year ago I fell off my bike near this house. I met Nick. He introduced me to his grandmother, Julia Jackson. She gave me a job, and I got to know the Jackson family. Julia kept tight control over her money. The family suffered. They were angry and frustrated. When Julia threatened to sell everything, take her money, and live in a hotel, the family was in shock."

"Yes," said Ronnie. "Tory and I heard them talking at dinner."

"That is true," said Tory. "Olivia said *everyone will be penniless and homeless.* Edgar said *we all want that old woman dead.* Victor said *with Julia's medical issues it was a surprise she was still alive.* And Nick said *insulin shock, a bee sting, or one of Tami's peanut butter sandwiches would do the trick.*"

"The following days were tense," said Tami. "Eva's and Nick's dreams were shattered. Kayla screamed in her bedroom. Edgar suffered in silence. Victor and Olivia quarreled. Olivia cried, 'Your mother can't keep me from my destiny!'"

Tory and Ronnie looked at each other. "That's true," said Tory.

"Ronnie ran out the house one morning," said Tami. "Ronnie screamed that Julia died. The doctor said that Julia's heart stopped. Julia's death changed the future for her family. Everyone's mood lifted right away. The wait for the money was over. Nick said *blue skies ahead*. I was shocked. The timing of her death seemed very, very suspicious to me."

"You wondered about Julia's allergies. You talked to the doctor and to Ronnie and me," said Tory.

"Yes," said Tami. "The doctor insisted Julia died of old age. But I was not satisfied. I searched the bedrooms, and I gathered information. I found plans the family had for the future. Plans that needed money—Julia's money. Plans that would not come to pass if Julia carried out her threat."

"That does not mean we killed Julia," said Eva.

Tami continued. "I visited the sheriff. He would not listen to me. He told me I was imagining things. Afterward, your family questioned me."

"You were interfering in a family matter," said Nick.

Eva nodded. "We wanted to get on with our lives."

"What happened then?" asked Tory.

"What could I do? Everyone insisted Julia died of old age. The doctor said her heart stopped. All I had were my suspicions. The Jacksons got Julia's money. They began their new lives. Nick, you and Eva plunged into plans for the Jackson Inn. Kayla went to California. Olivia joined the research lab in Costa Rica. Victor and Edgar followed her."

Tami continued. "I decided to complete the photo project and leave. Then one afternoon, I found an internet article hidden in a book in the estate office. It was titled 'Allergies and Death.' The article explained that some deaths from allergies do not leave any trace. The person who read that article could have caused Julia's death. But who was it?"

CHAPTER 17

WHO KILLED JULIA?

"What kind of person killed Julia Jackson? A picture of the murderer formed in my mind. A careful person. A determined person. A ruthless person. A person who let *nothing and no one* stand in their way. A person with only one thing in mind—themself."

Tami smiled at Eva. "Eva, you wept about leaving your garden. You are too gentle to kill someone. You are not capable of murder. I also eliminated Kayla and Edgar. They did not have the patience."

Tami turned to Nick. "I was not sure about you, Nick. You are clever.

Your grandmother stood in the way of your dream. But you were not a bitter person."

Tami frowned. "It was either Victor or Olivia. They both wanted to get away from Julia. They needed a lot of money to do it. They were both angry. And frustrated. And bitter."

"Maybe they did it together," suggested Tory.

"I thought of that," said Tami. "But in the end, I decided the murder was the work of one person."

She opened *Murderers and Their Personalities*. She took out the envelope. Eva, Nick, Tory, and Ronnie crowded around.

"In this envelope is the name of the murderer. Here, Nick, you read it."

"The murderer is Oliva Jackson!"

"Olivia! Not Victor!" cried Eva.

"No," said Tami. "Victor was miserable, but he remembered happy family times. I did not think he would kill his mother."

Tami explained more. "Of all the members of the Jackson family, Olivia had the murderer's personality. 'The lab in Costa Rica recognizes the important work that I do. I am entitled to realize my ambitions. Your mother can't keep me from my destiny. I will find a way to get to Costa Rica.' These were Olivia's words."

Tami frowned. "There was more. Olivia said, 'Maybe Tami's job here should come to an end.' Then I had a dangerous bike accident. I could have been killed. Someone wanted to get rid of me."

"These are just guesses," said Nick. "None of this is proof that Olivia killed Julia."

Tami placed the newspaper on the table. "Read this," she said.

STRANGE DEATH STILL A MYSTERY!

Victor Jackson, an American, has died. Mr. Jackson ate a death apple. It is the poisonous fruit of a tree called the Tree of Death. No one knows how Mr. Jackson ate this deadly fruit. Mr. Jackson is survived by his wife, the well-known scientist Olivia Jackson. "I will build my own laboratory with the money from Victor's life insurance," said

Mrs. Jackson. "I will call it the Victor Jackson Laboratory. I think my dear husband would have liked that."

"Victor is dead," cried Eva. "Why didn't Olivia notify us?"

"I will explain," answered Tami. "Only one person fit the profile of a murderer. That person was Olivia. Olivia would not let anyone stand in her way. Olivia needed money, so Julia had to die. Olivia read about deaths from allergies. She crept into Julia's bedroom and killed her. Then Olivia had the money for Costa Rica. But when she got there, she was still not satisfied. She wanted more. She wanted her own private science lab. She needed more money. Oliva specialized in poisonous plants. I am sure she knew about the death apple. She killed once for money, so she killed a second time. This time it was her husband, Victor.

"I could not let Olivia get away with murder again. I emailed the police in Costa Rica. I told them about the events leading up to Julia Jackson's death."

Tami placed one more document on the table. "Here is their response."

"Dear Ms. Tripper. Thank you for your email. We confirmed your suspicions about the death of Victor Jackson. As a result, Olivia Jackson has been arrested for the murder of her husband. We are sure she will be convicted of the crime."

"Poor Victor," whispered Eva.

"And poor Julia," added Nick. "She

was hard to live with, but she should not have been murdered. Tami, we misjudged you. You questioned Julia's death. We all ignored you. But you persisted. You did not give up. And you were right. A murder occurred in this house. When Julia hired you she said, 'I like your independent spirit.' That independent spirit brought her killer to justice. How can we repay you?" asked Nick.

"Nick, there is nothing to repay. I am a curious person. I had to solve the puzzle of how Julia died. After all, my mother called me Ms. Nosy!"